COLLATERAL
DAMAGE

SUPPORT AND DEFEND

COLLATERAL DAMAGE

PATRICK JONES & BRENT CHARTIER

darby creek

MINNEAPOLIS

The authors wish to thank Susan Olson, Professional Counselor, M.Ed., LPC, for her expertise on military families and thoughtful review of manuscripts in the Support and Defend series.

Darby Creek
A division of Lerner Publishing Group, Inc.
241 First Avenue North
Minneapolis, MN 55401 USA

For reading levels and more information, look up this title at
www.lernerbooks.com.

Cover and Interior photographs, © David Ellis/Aurora Photos/CORBIS (man); © iStockphoto.com/mart_m (dog tags); © iStockphoto.com/ CollinsChin (background).

Main body text set in Janson Text LT Std 12/17.5.
Typeface provided by Adobe Systems.

Library of Congress Cataloging-in-Publication Data

Jones, Patrick, 1961–
    Collateral Damage / by Patrick Jones and Brent Chartier.
        p. cm. — (Support and defend)
    Summary: Ty is very proud of his father's accomplishments as a U.S. Army sergeant, but when a brain injury and partial paralysis send his father home from Afghanistan in a wheelchair, Ty finds it hard to balance schoolwork, basketball, a girlfriend, and friends with the time and effort required to care for him.
    ISBN 978-1-4677-8050-6 (lb : alk. paper)
    ISBN 978-1-4677-8091-9 (pb : alk. paper)
    ISBN 978-1-4677-8818-2 (eb pdf : alk. paper)
    [1. Fathers and sons—Fiction. 2. People with disabilities—Fiction.
3. Basketball—Fiction. 4. High schools—Fiction. 5. Schools—Fiction.
6. Soldiers—Fiction.] I. Chartier, Brent. II. Title.
PZ7.J7242Col 2015
[Fic]—dc23   2015000593

Manufactured in the United States of America
1 – SB – 7/15/15

TO THE BRAVE MEN AND WOMEN
IN THE US MILITARY AND THE
FAMILIES THAT SUPPORT THEM
—P.J. AND B.C.

∎

DECEMBER 27 / SATURDAY EVENING
WAYNE STATE UNIVERSITY FIELD HOUSE, DETROIT, MI

Fifteen seconds and a 56–56 tie on the scoreboard.

Tyshawn dribbled down court, head faking and cutting past his opposing guard. Cass Tech's star center stood five feet in front, arms outstretched, ready to block Ty if he rushed the post.

From the corner of his eye, Ty saw Arquavis drawing a double team. No one else who could shoot worth anything was open either.

Good thing Dad wasn't in the stands, thought Ty. He could just hear his father saying, *You're the point guard, Ty, you're captain. Your job is to run the offense, not be the offense. Sacrifice your shots for the good of the team.*

9 seconds.

Arquavis pushed off, but Cass Tech's coverage held.

7 seconds.

Tyshawn had to act, think, and decide fast. The hulking Cass Tech center lurched forward.

5 seconds.

Ty turned and jumped sideways for the open shot, off balance, and let the ball fly.

Ty fell to the floor as the ball sailed up.

3 seconds.

Too high, thought Ty, being as hard on himself as his father. But it wasn't. In fact, the shot was perfect.

2 seconds.

The ball sank through the net. A three-pointer.

The buzzer sounded. The crowd roared as the Warren High Wildcats won the Hungry Howie's Holiday Basketball Tournament for the second straight year.

With Ty still on the floor, his teammates cleared the bench and court and piled on—a four-foot-high pile of the best players in the city, Ty at the bottom.

"Nice shot, man!"

"Way to go, Ty!"

"Great job, Teflon!" He'd earned that nickname by claiming no defender could stick to him.

Ty could hear the crowd in the stands, "Ty! Ty! Ty!"

A large hand reached in and pulled Ty from the pile of players. It was Coach Carlson. "Great shot, Tyshawn! Way to think out there!" Coach shouted over the crowd.

Ty glanced at the off-court celebration. Leading it was Shania, the cutest cheerleader on the Wildcats squad, in Ty's opinion. Though being her boyfriend made Ty biased.

He grabbed a towel from the bench, wiped sweat from his face, and winked at Shania. Shania blew him a kiss.

Arquavis saw it as well. "You get the game *and* the girl, since you wouldn't pass me the ball?" he asked Ty. "They should be cheering me," Arquavis said in his best playground trash-talking tone. That had been the plan, but in the last seconds with Arquavis double-teamed, Ty felt he could handle the pressure. Ty narrowed his eyes at the verbal slap, but he couldn't wipe the smile from his face.

The announcer spoke over the PA system. "Congratulations to our tournament champions, the Warren Wildcats!" With that, Ty waved the towel over his head, whipping the crowd to an even higher frenzy.

Coach Carlson came over to Ty as two older white guys in suits carried the trophy to a table at center court. "Follow me," said Coach.

Ty thought how proud his dad would be

when Ty showed him that giant, shiny trophy. But his father's return from Afghanistan was deferred, again. He'd been first scheduled to return in the fall, but the days of delay fell like dominos. All Ty knew was his dad got concussed and was recuperating in a hospital in Germany.

One of the white guys handed Ty the trophy. "Nice job, Son," said the man.

Son. Ty was ready to hear that more often. This time when his dad came home, it would be for good. No more deployments. Ty lifted the trophy above his head.

The announcer spoke. "If I can direct your attention to the big screen, we have a special announcement for the most valuable player of today's game, Tyshawn Douglas. Please join me in welcoming, all the way from a military hospital in Landstuhl, Germany, Tyshawn's father, Sergeant Denver Douglas of the United States Army!"

The crowd hushed. Ty saw his father all right, sitting up in a hospital bed, tubes running from his arms, a bandage covering half his head. "How did this—?" Ty asked his coach.

His coach whispered, "I got connections, and you deserve it. I knew with your hard work, you had a big game in you."

"Ty," his father started, slowly, weakly. "Congratu—lations—Son—I—am—so—proud." The crowd cheered, but not a word came out of Ty's mouth. It was the first time he'd seen his father in months. On his father's last mission on his last deployment this summer, he'd been wounded. Now here he was, Denver Douglas, as big as a house, up on the screen.

Ty set the trophy down. He covered his face with the towel, now wet with both sweat and tears.

2

Ty didn't wait until the ball dropped in Times Square to kiss Shania; he didn't need an excuse. Their first kiss had happened exactly one year earlier at a New Year's party thrown by a senior on the team. They'd hardly come up for air since then.

"You sure you're okay with this?" Ty whispered. The two were curled up on the sofa in Ty's basement in front of the big-screen TV. "There are lots of parties we can go to."

Shania cut him off with another kiss. "I don't want to be anywhere else but with you."

"I just don't feel like being in a crowd," Ty said. At six-foot-five, Ty almost always stood out, especially when he was with the six-foot Shania. With a wild streak of Wildcats purple in her hair, Shania attracted attention—sometimes too much for Ty's taste.

"You nervous about your dad?"

Ty reached for the remote and paused the DVD of Bruce Lee's *Enter the Dragon*. He and his father knew every Bruce Lee film by heart. On the screen, Bruce Lee stood frozen, mouth open but silent, just like Ty. He didn't know what to say; this wasn't a simple yes-or-no question.

"Ty?"

"Mom's seen him, and she said he's kind of messed up." Ty stumbled over his words.

Shania nodded. "I saw that in the video too."

"But this is my dad we're talking about here, Shania." Ty's voice grew stronger. "He is a living, breathing hero. I think Mom's just trying to make excuses. She does that a lot."

"Is he going to be okay?"

"Sure 'nuff. Mom says I'll need to help him some, but Dad's got this. I know it."

"What's he like?" Shania asked. Ty's father was deployed to Afghanistan a few months before Shania entered Ty's world.

"Let me show you." Ty left the sofa. He dangled his long fingers behind. Shania intertwined her fingers with his and followed him to a corner of the basement.

On the wall were the two careers of Denver Douglas as told in framed photos. The first set of photographs was of Denver Douglas, high school basketball star and freshman star forward on scholarship to Eastern Michigan. But no photos of what he thought would follow: a pro career. A set of bad knees, ruined from years of pick-up ball on the hard, cracked cement of Detroit playgrounds coupled with a crippling ACL tear in his junior year ended his basketball career before it really started.

Then, photos of his dad's second career. "That's from basic," Ty pointed at his father in uniform. He didn't explain the ten years difference between the end of his basketball career and the start of his military service. Ty remembered moving a lot around Detroit, sometimes at a moment's notice before the landlord evicted them for not paying the rent, leaving most of his belongings behind. That all changed when his dad joined the Army. It gave him more than a job; it gave him stability. "He just looks right in that uniform, don't you think?"

Shania nodded, but Ty was already back to studying the photos. Each one showed a new rank, from a private to a sergeant, and with it a new confidence. Ty saw in the pictures how the Army had given his father self-assurance, purpose, and a sense of being part of something larger, even if it often took him away from their family.

And with each deployment, Ty's tension had increased, always fearing the call every military family feared, informing him his small family had gotten smaller.

"You're so proud of him," Shania wrapped her arms around Ty's neck.

"More than I can say." His dad was another step closer to home, at Dingell, the VA Hospital in downtown Detroit. His mom had told him his dad wasn't ready yet for a visit from Ty, so they'd just talked on the phone. But Ty did most of the talking. Like on the video, his dad spoke slowly, like each word hurt. Ty wondered what else about his father would be different.

"When's he coming home?" Shania asked.

"Next week, unless there's another delay."

"I can't wait to meet him."

Ty stopped himself from saying "me too." Even from the few seconds of grainy video feed after the tournament win and the hour or so of difficult phone calls, Ty could tell his dad had changed again. Maybe it would be like meeting a new person. The Army gave his dad everything, but what had it taken in return?

3

Ty stared out the window of the school bus as it rounded the corner and came to a stop in front of his house, its brakes squealing. Ty hated taking the bus, but he didn't have much choice, seeing as he didn't have money to buy gas for his dad's old Ford.

"Way cool, Teflon. You got a skateboard ramp on your house," said Demonte, a skinny skater kid sitting in front of him.

Ty watched from the bus window as three men, two in army fatigues, nail-gunned boards of lumber to a ramp that ran from the porch to the driveway.

"Skateboard ramp?" said Ty aloud. "I don't skateboard."

"We'll be over tonight," said Benj, another skater. "Once it snows, it'll be too icy."

"I'll check it out," said Ty as he exited the bus and walked up the driveway.

One of the men met Ty halfway down the driveway. "You must be Tyshawn," he said.

"Yes, sir," said Ty. "Is that a skateboard ramp?"

The man took his hat off and laughed. "No, but I suppose it could be," said the man. "That's for your father's wheelchair."

Ty's heart sank in his chest. *Wheelchair?* he thought. *Nobody said anything about Dad being in a wheelchair.*

At that moment, Ty's mom called from the front door. "Tyshawn, come quick. I need you."

Ty started for the door, but the man reached for his shoulder and stopped him. "Young man, tell your father welcome home, would you, please?"

"Yes, and give him our thanks for his service," said another of the workers.

"Yes, sir."

Ty made his way to the front door. When he stepped inside, his mother was putting in earrings. She spoke quickly. These days, it seemed like she was always in a hurry.

"Your father's home," she said, "but I got called to work. There's a truck at the Canadian border they're not letting through, and it's costing the company money."

Before Ty was born, his mother took a job at an auto parts supplier that had grown to become one of the largest in the country. As the company grew, so did her responsibilities.

"Can I say hi to Dad?"

"When I'm gone," she said, sounding almost out of breath. "I've got lots to show you."

She led Ty to the kitchen. "These are his medications," she said, pointing to a row of orange pill bottles. "He takes one of these a half hour before dinner. This one," she said, pointing to another bottle, "before bed. Don't get them confused or you'll throw his schedule off."

Ty followed her to the bathroom, which had been fitted with a toilet seat adjuster and a shower seat. "They just put this in," she said. "He can't stand to shower anymore, so if he wants to take one, you have to help him to his seat."

"Help him to—" Ty began, but his mother interrupted.

"It's a struggle for him to stand after sitting, so this height adjuster should help."

Ty swallowed. He was impatient to see his father again, but the image of helping him to the shower and toilet took some of the excitement away.

She led Ty to the living room.

"What's with the furniture?" asked Ty.

"We had to move it so he could get his wheelchair through," she said, matter-of-factly. "Now, let me show you your room."

She led Ty to what had been his bedroom. In the room, his father lay, sleeping on a hospital bed.

"Where's my—" began Ty.

"We had to move your bedroom downstairs," interrupted his mother, whispering so as not to wake her husband. "There are just too many machines for our bedroom."

She was right. Where Ty's desk had been, there was a machine with a large fan in front. Where Ty's bookcase had been was a wheelchair. And in place of the dresser was another machine and a tall device with a swing attached. The Fatheads on his walls had been replaced by charts and a wipe board. His bedroom looked like a clinic.

"How'd you get everything moved?" Ty whispered.

"The volunteer vets outside, building the ramp, they moved everything this morning.

They also threw a little welcome party for your father. I had an important call from work. Otherwise, I would have picked you up from school for it. But the good thing is, there's plenty of food in the fridge."

She turned her attention to the room. "This is his lift. For him to get out of bed, plug this in. Here are the controls. You bring the wheelchair over, lift him up, then set him in his chair. When he wants back in bed, do what I just said in reverse. Got it?"

"It's a bit—"

"You'll figure it out." She kissed Ty quickly on the forehead. With one arm on his shoulder, she paused as she looked into Ty's eyes and spoke. "Your dad's home now. Home for good. But our lives will never be the same." She patted Ty on the cheek and left the room. A moment later, he heard the front door close.

Ty looked around his bedroom—what *had been* his bedroom—at the machines and the large, blue hospital bed where his dad was sleeping.

4

"Ty? Ty?" His father turned his head, his eyes half open.

"Dad, you're home," said Ty, leaning down for a hug.

"Not too hard, son. I still . . . hurt quite a bit."

Ty stood up. Of the many things his father had been, frail wasn't one of them.

"Where's your mother?"

"She had to go back to work. Something came up . . . she said."

Ty's father paused for a moment, like he was collecting his thoughts. "Could you help me get . . . out of bed? I need . . . to use the bathroom."

Ty knew he didn't have a choice—he was the only one there to help his father now. Trouble was, his mother's instructions weren't the best.

With his father directing him in sentences full of long pauses, Ty brought the body swing over and lowered it next to the bed. He then brought the wheelchair over.

It took some doing, but Ty lifted his father onto the wheelchair and pushed him to the bathroom.

"Where's your mother again?" his dad asked. Ty thought he sounded confused.

"Dad, I told you, she had to go to work."

"I just don't have the memory I used to . . . I got hit in the head . . . pretty bad."

The bathroom was less of a challenge. Once past the door, Ty's father said he could handle it from there, so Ty shut the door and went downstairs.

The basement—now his bedroom—was a mess with clothes, books, and furniture stacked and piled everywhere. Ty took a deep sigh and started to arrange things before he heard his father call him. Ty rushed upstairs.

"There you are. I thought . . . I thought . . . you'd gone off to school."

"School's been over for hours."

Ty's father dropped his head. "Ha. Time flies."

Ty wheeled his father into the living room, next to the couch.

"Can you fix dinner tonight, son? I'm just a little . . . off," said his father, laughing.

This wasn't a good development. "Dad, I'm no cook, you know that." Just then, he remembered. "But Mom said there are leftovers from the party." The party he'd missed.

As he took a quick inventory of the tubs and bowls in the refrigerator, his father shouted from the living room. "What would Bruce Lee have for dinner? What was that movie?" Ty tried to remember the name of the film where the martial arts actor had ordered four large bowls of soup. "I can't remember the movie, Dad."

"Welcome to the club," Ty's dad laughed. Ty never even cracked a smile.

* * *

A half hour later, Ty and his father were seated at the kitchen table, scraping their dinner plates clean of beans, salad, and fried chicken.

Ty's phone rang. It was his mother.

"Did you remember the medication he's supposed to have before dinner?" she asked.

Ty shot up from his chair, "Crap!"

He rushed to the pill bottles.

There was a knock at the door.

Ty went to the door and opened it, his phone in hand.

"The ramp's finished," said one of the workers. "Give your dad our best."

"I will. Thank you."

Ty went back to the pill bottles, his mother still on the phone.

"I told you, he has to have that medication before dinner or it will upset his stomach."

"Upset? What does that mean?"

"He'll vomit, that's what it means."

There was another knock at the door.

"We waited for the old guys to leave." It was Benj and Demonte, kids from the bus, each with a skateboard in hand. "Can we skate your ramp, man?"

Before he could answer, Ty heard his father make an odd noise, just before he heard the ugly sound of vomit hitting the floor.

Ty's shoulders dropped. There were dishes to put away, homework to do, and his bedroom lay in piles on the basement floor. And now there was a mess to clean.

5

Ty's white Jordans smacked hard against the brown bleacher stairs Coach Carlson made him run after practice. He'd seen his teammates, Arquavis in particular, run those stairs as punishment for being late for practice. But for him, it was a first. His mind raced to the first dinner he'd made the night before and that he'd been up way too late, cleaning up after his father's upset stomach—another first. His mom had been tied up at work all night—not a first.

"Tyshawn, see me when you're done," Coach Carlson shouted. He'd shouted at Ty most of the way through practice. The more Coach shouted, the more Ty pressed. The more he pressed, the more Ty made the wrong pass, the wide shot, or set a bad screen.

"Yes, sir," Ty shouted back, not wanting to show he felt winded.

"And don't be late again, Tyshawn!"

One more "yes sir," one more flight of stairs, one more obstacle. As he sweated under the hot lights of the gym, Ty knew his friends were showering off, getting dressed, and getting on with their lives. He wasn't on point, he was left behind. But it had been like that all day, what with missing so much sleep the night before.

As he descended the bleachers for the tenth and final time, Ty felt nothing but guilt. *What am I complaining about?* he thought. He knew this was nothing compared to what his dad went through—or what he was going through now. *Man up, Ty, man up.*

"Done, Coach," Ty said. Coach Carlson motioned for Ty to sit next to him. Coach Carlson was shorter than Ty, but somehow he seemed larger. Like some guys in school or at playground pick-up games—and Ty's dad—Coach owned the space he occupied.

"Why were you late?" Coach asked.

Ty studied the hard wood under his feet at the same time he fought back a yawn. "It won't happen again."

"That's not what I asked."

Ty didn't know what to say. No way Coach could understand what was happening at home. He knew Ty's dad had been injured; what he didn't know was that his injuries made his dad a different person. After other deployments, Ty's dad mostly left the war behind. Maybe he was a little different in ways that were hard to describe. But this time, he'd brought the war home like an unwanted gift.

"Whatever's going on, Tyshawn, you know the rule," Coach said. "Two more tardies and you're off the team. Got it?"

Ty tugged on the frayed end of his practice uniform. He knew that without basketball, he could just as easily have been wearing another set of colors, like so many of the guys he'd gone to school with over the years. He had the hard wood, they had the harder streets.

"It won't happen again," Ty assured his coach.

"Don't let your teammates down," Coach said. "Now, go get dressed."

Ty sprinted to the locker room. Before hitting the showers, he pulled out his phone. Four missed calls: Shania, Shania, Shania, and Shania. No messages. That was a message itself. Ty put a towel over his head and the phone to his ear.

Shania picked up on the fifth try. "Where are you?"

"I'm sorry. I had to stay after practice." On Wednesdays, cheerleading practice ended the same time as basketball. Last season, and so far this season, Ty and Shania drove home together, usually in Shania's ride. It was as ingrained a habit as getting to practice on time.

"I've been waiting for hours."

Ty didn't correct her as he looked at the time on his phone. He was twenty minutes late, although he knew how time slowed down while waiting on someone. "I'm sorry."

"Tyshawn, are you coming or not?" Shania snapped.

"Let me get showered and dressed. I'll be right there."

Shania didn't answer. Her silence felt like a shot block.

"Come on. It's only the first time I've been late."

More silence before Shania answered. "Then get yourself out here," she said, sounding less sour. "It's cold, Boo."

"Sure enough," Ty said as he hung up. Before he put his phone back in the locker, he stared at the pic of Shania and him at Homecoming, all dressed up, all smiles. Like the photos of his dad in the basement, the photo captured a moment in time when everything was a promise of tomorrow. Ty worried if he didn't hold it together, Shania—like the father in the photos—would be nothing more than a memory.

6

JANUARY 9 / FRIDAY MORNING
WARREN HIGH SCHOOL

Ty looked at the red D scrawled on his math test.

"See me after class," Mr. Murry whispered, his coffee breath wafting over Ty.

"Sure enough, Mr. M.," Ty answered with a yawn. No wonder he was making D's on tests when he couldn't get any Z's at night.

As Mr. Murry handed out the other papers, Ty sent a quick text to Shania, who was sitting in the front row of the class.

Ty's text read, simply, "D."

He waited for her response, then looked up to see her whispering something to Arquavis who sat in the seat next to her. Ty felt like sending Arquavis a message with his phone by throwing it against his thick skull and knocking the smirk off his face. The bell rang to end class before he got his chance, or before Shania replied.

"Yes, Mr. M.?" Ty said, waiting until everyone had cleared the classroom.

Mr. Murry sat behind his desk in front of the room. Ty stayed in his seat, way too small for his big frame. Twenty feet and thousands of experiences separated them.

"You're better than this, Tyshawn," said Mr. Murry.

"I know," Ty agreed. His dad had taught him well: respect authority. *Arguing with teachers and coaches never gets you where you wanna be.*

"You want to talk about anything?"

"No."

"You want to talk to your counselor?" Mr. Murry asked. He stole a quick glance at his computer. "It's Mrs. Howard, right?"

"Yes."

"I could send her a message and you could—"

"No."

Ty wondered why everything couldn't be so simple: yes and no answers, X's and O's on Coach's wipe board. "There's a tutoring group after school that—"

"I have basketball."

"Not if you don't keep your grades up," Mr. Murry said in a slap-in-the-face tone. Unlike teachers who didn't push Ty and other players, Mr. Murry seemed to delight in failing athletes. Ty hadn't even wanted to take Mr. Murry's class, but he'd gotten Coach to change his schedule since Shania was in the class. He regretted the change since he'd been shooting bricks on every test and quiz so far.

"Tyshawn, I want you to do well in my class, in all your classes," Mr. Murry said, as if he could sense Ty's resentment. "You need to work hard in order to succeed."

Tyshawn wanted to shout, *Work? You don't know how hard I work at home!*

"Everybody knows what happened to your father, but I know you don't want to let him down, either—or Coach Carlson or the team," Mr. Murry added as Ty's resentment grew hotter, deeper. "You'd better get to your next class," Mr. Murry said.

Just days ago, people had chanted his name and cheered for him like a hero. Now, yet another D on yet another quiz. Ty got up, tossed the quiz into the trash, and left the room feeling like a loser.

7

Not again, thought Ty as he stood on the porch.

Beyond the door, he heard shouting. His mother's voice loud and firm. "You can, but you don't even try!"

Then came his father's voice, the exact opposite—low, small. "I did try."

"Then try harder! There's too much going on at work for me to take care of everything—EVERYTHING!"

Ty heard a crash.

"Look what you made me do!" his mother's voice came across loud and clear.

Ty took a deep breath and opened the door.

The scene was just like the past two nights when he'd come home in the middle of his parents arguing. His father sat in his wheel-chair at the dinner table, facing the door, his face blank.

What was different today was his mother, who was on her knees on the kitchen floor, pick-ing up pieces of broken glass. She looked up.

"Just where have you been?!" she shouted.

Ty swallowed. "Basketball practice, like every night after school."

His mom stopped long enough to rest her forehead against the palm of one hand. "That's right. I knew that," she said in a softer tone. Ty didn't mention playing lip one-on-one with Shania after practice.

"Hi, Dad, Mom."

"Hello, Ty," said his dad, but his mother

wasn't through with the argument.

She leaned against her heels as she spoke in a matter-of-fact tone. "You tell me you can't take care of yourself. Well, I can't either. I have to work and do a hundred things around this house. And frankly, Denver, I'm tired."

It was Ty's dad's turn to grow angry. "You think I want to be this way?!"

Ty had had enough. He carried his books downstairs and flipped the basement light on to be greeted by Fatheads of Ty Lawson and LeBron James on the opposite wall. "Hey, guys," he whispered as he set his books down. "Have they been at this long?" He waited a moment. "That so?" he replied to an imaginary answer. "Any bets how long this will last? They argued past midnight last night."

Just then, Ty's father called to him from the kitchen. Ty headed upstairs.

He reached the kitchen to find his mother with her arm outstretched in warning. "Do not do what he asks, Ty. Do not!"

"So, your mother here says you're on kitchen duty. What are you fixin' for dinner?"

"Do not do this, Ty. He'll never get stronger if we baby him." The way his mom said *baby* made it sound worse than any swear word. Ty looked at his father.

"Please?" his dad said.

His mom leaned against the counter. She raised her gaze in his father's direction and spoke slowly. "You keep this up, Denver, and I swear I—will—leave."

* * *

As Ty cleaned up after dinner, his father spoke, his words not nearly as slow as when he was hooked up to machines during his holiday tournament videochat or in his first days home. "I feel better. Thank you, Ty. I was ready to eat my wheelchair."

"No problem, Dad."

"Your mom's right, I've got to do more. But these pills I'm on, they make me feel so loopy."

Ty loaded the dishwasher in silence.

"Your mom's just got so much on her mind. I'm glad she's sleeping now. She'll be okay."

Ty noticed a yellow note on the fridge: *Remind Ty. Vet Center group.*

"What's this, Dad?"

"Oh, glad I wrote it down. A Vet Center counselor called today. Said he wants to talk to you."

"A counselor?"

"He heads up a support group for teens whose folks are in combat. Said he wanted to see you at the next meeting, this Saturday."

Ty held the note in his hand. "Did he say what they do at these meetings?" Sitting around talking about things wasn't Ty's way; he was about action.

"He didn't. But there's one way to find out." He studied Ty's face. "Remember what Bruce Lee said about water?"

Ty remembered. *Water takes whatever direction or form it's given.* With basketball, grades, and his home life disrupted, Ty knew direction and form was exactly what he needed.

Ty looked into his father's face. At exactly the same moment, the two spoke—"Be water, my friend."

8

"So, you going in, or are you going to lean against the wall all day, holding it up?"

Ty had watched this girl walk the long hallway of the Vet Center. With her short, cropped hair, big smile, and an orange dress with a green scarf, she stood out in the hallway full of men and women going about their business.

Now, here she was, talking to him as he stood outside a doorway marked "Teen ACHIEVE."

"What?" asked Ty.

She placed a hand on her hip. "This room is the teen support group. I'm guessing that's why you're here. Or maybe your job is to just lean against this wall, hoping it won't fall." She paused. "Or maybe the wall's holding *you* up so *you* won't fall, and if that's the case, then you need this support group more than you know."

"I'm late. I didn't want to interrupt the group."

"You won't be." She reached for his hand. "Here, I'm Malayeka."

She opened the door, but Ty let her go in first.

The room held a circle of maybe thirty chairs, most of them filled with teens. A Hispanic-looking guy with one of the biggest smiles Ty had ever seen jumped from his chair and rushed over when he saw Malayeka.

"Malayeka," he said. "So glad you could make it." The man turned to Ty. "And you brought a guest."

Ty spoke softly. "My name's Tyshawn."

"Great! Your father gave you my message,"

he said, still smiling. "I'm Mr. Gomez. Welcome to Teen ACHIEVE. Have a seat."

Ty and Malayeka took chairs next to each other as Mr. Gomez spoke.

"Welcome, Tyshawn. I'll give a quick introduction to the group. Everyone here has a parent in the military or who is a vet. Some have a parent wounded in combat. That can be a big change in our lives, so Teen ACHIEVE is a safe place to share what's going on and learn ways to adjust."

"You forgot about me, Mr. Gomez," one of the teens spoke up. The teen looked at Ty. "My dad *died* in combat. He didn't even get a chance to get wounded."

Mr. Gomez spoke. "That's right. I'm sorry, Tori. To help with the tremendous change in your life—as a teenager—that's why I started Teen ACHIEVE. Glad you're here."

At Mr. Gomez's request, everyone in the circle introduced themselves and why they were there. More than a handful had a parent with a head injury, like Ty's dad. Some teens shared the details—bomb blasts, mostly. Ty figured when it was time, his dad would share the details of his injury too.

It was Ty's turn. "I'm Ty. Um, my dad's having a hard time."

"With what?" Tori asked.

Ty tried not to stare at Malayeka. It was a challenge. "With everything," Ty answered. "He still can't do much for himself."

Malayeka spoke. "Your mom's having a tough time, too, isn't she?"

Ty looked at her, surprised, but didn't speak.

"It's the same with all of us, Ty. The adjustment—it's hard on everyone. And I bet your coach sees it, too."

"You know Coach Carlson?"

"No, but I recognize the guy that made the three-pointer in the last seconds of the Holiday Tournament." Malayeka smiled. "I go to Cass Tech. I was in the stands."

9

"There's so much to keep track of," Ty told the group, settled in after a half hour of listening to others.

Mr. Gomez leaned forward and nodded. "That's true, Ty. So tell us about one or two things that cause a problem for you. Maybe someone in the group has a solution."

Ty looked around the room, his gaze landing on a smiling Malayeka.

"Alright," said Ty, "his pills." He counted on his fingers. "He's takes one before dinner, then—"

"Use the alarm on his cell phone," interrupted a girl named Queen. "If he takes one at three o'clock, set the alarm for three and use the text feature to tell him what medication it is."

A grin grew slowly across Ty's face. "You're kiddin' me?"

Mr. Gomez took over. "It's an easy solution to a hard problem. But it works."

"He takes five meds," said Ty.

"So set five alarms," Queen said.

Ty thought. "But what if he's nowhere near his phone?"

"Phone belt," said Alicia, a cute white girl with spikey red hair. "My mom made this thing out of a cell phone case and a belt. My dad always has his phone."

Ty laughed, "You guys have thought of everything."

"We've had to," said Alicia, although she wasn't laughing.

Ty checked himself. "I'm sorry, I wasn't laughing at you. It's just, I never would have thought of that myself."

Alicia continued. "Are meals a problem?"

"How'd you know?"

Mr. Gomez smiled. "That's why we have the support group. To share—share emotions, frustrations, ideas."

Alicia continued. "Sunday night, Mom and I make meals for the week. We freeze them in containers with labels so he knows which container to use on which day. For snacks, we keep peanut butter sandwiches in the refrigerator."

"Wow," said Ty.

"And we set the alarm for when he's supposed to eat. Some brain damaged people don't even know when they're hungry."

Ty felt punched in the gut. He'd thought of his father lots of different ways: athlete, coach, Army sergeant, hero, struggling injured vet. He wasn't "brain damaged." Was he?

* * *

Ty took the bus home from the Vet Center. Everyone on the bus was in their own little world full of problems, although Teen ACHIEVE showed him he wasn't alone. After the group, Mr. Gomez had shared handouts with more ideas and invited him to the next group. As for Malayeka, she had left him with a smile and, "Hope to see you again, Ty."

Once home, he found his dad watching a Bruce Lee movie.

"Great. You came in at the best part," he said.

"Where's Mom?" asked Ty as he sat on the couch, Mr. Gomez's handouts in his hand.

"Your mom? Here, watch," his father said, pointing at the screen. "This is the first time Bruce fights the bad guys."

"He's always fightin' bad guys, Dad."

"Not in this movie."

Ty watched the first few kicks, then looked down at the handouts and read. *Post Concussion Syndrome: What Is It? 10 Tips to Better Caregiving.*

On the screen, Bruce Lee had just knocked out a bad guy and then sat on his body.

"Dad, where's Mom?"

Ty's father lifted the remote to lower the volume, but accidently turned it up instead. The sounds of kicks and punches filled the room. Ty grabbed the remote and paused it.

His dad looked at him. "Your mom, she wants to take some time away. It's a stressful time for her, so she left."

Ty jumped up. "What do you mean, *left*?"

"She's staying with a friend."

Ty felt like he was on the receiving end of a Bruce Lee kick. "She'll be back, right?" More silence from his father. "Dad?" Ty asked.

His father stared at the screen and shrugged. "I don't know. I'm not the husband I used to be." He looked at Ty. "I know I'm not the father I was, either. When it gets to be too much, for survival, it's fight or flight. You either fight or get out of there. Your mom has to decide what she wants to do."

Ty looked around the room, shocked that his mom just up and left.

"Don't worry, Son. We can do this. We're fighters, right?"

Ty dropped his arms to his side.

"Look, I have good news."

With that, his father gripped hard the arms of his wheelchair and slowly lifted himself up. Once out of the chair, he took six steps. "What do you think? They picked me up for physical therapy today. Said I should be at twenty steps next week. Before you know it, we'll be playing one-on-one again."

Ty glanced at the screen, at Bruce Lee, the fighter. He looked at his father, the sergeant who called the steps in battle, now fighting to learn to walk again.

"Yeah, we can do this," Ty said, making fists with his hands, "'cause we're fighters."

10

"Ten more minutes, Tyshawn!" Coach Carlson yelled over the sound of the ball bouncing off the backboard, away from the net. Ty missed the shoot-around at the start of practice, late again. His dad had called in a panic, needing Ty to take the school bus home. When Ty got home, his dad forgot why he'd called.

Ty gassed up the Ford with a fistful of change and drove back to school for practice, but he was too late. Coach greeted Ty by making him run the bleachers and then stay longer for shooting practice alone.

Another shot, another miss. Ty thought, *If I don't get my game together, I'll be sitting on the bench like some civilian.*

Coach Carlson shook his head as he tossed loose basketballs from the gym floor in Ty's direction. From just outside the three-point range, Ty launched three quick shots. The clang of the balls hitting the rim echoed through the empty gym. *That's my life now,* Ty thought, *the sounds of clanging backboards, Coach's complaints, and beeping machines.* He missed the sounds of nothing but net and Shania's whispers. Ty gripped the round, orange ball tighter and shut his eyes tighter still.

"Don't overthink it. Trust yourself." Coach Carlson patted Ty on the back.

"Balance, that's what I need," Ty said, his father's words ringing in his ears.

Ty took a deep breath and exhaled as the

ball sailed through the air, Ty and the ball making the same swishing sound as Coach Carlson applauded.

* * *

"Not much of a date," Shania said as she put the last grocery bag in the trunk.

"Sorry," Ty mumbled. Shania wanted more of his time than he could give lately, taking care of his dad. Add in school and ball, and twenty-four hours in a day didn't cut it anymore.

"You've been saying 'sorry' a lot."

"Sorry." Ty laughed, but Shania narrowed her eyes like a sniper taking aim.

"How'd you do on Murry's quiz?" Shania asked as they climbed in the car. She'd loaned him money for gas. He'd been more scared asking her for that than asking her to prom last year.

"C." Another mumble.

"I got an A," Shania said, rubbing it in like she wanted to punish him for ignoring her. "If you'd study more with me, you wouldn't be getting C's."

Ty said nothing as they drove to his house in silence, sticking to the speed limit. Not too fast, not too slow. Just follow the rules. Balance. Balance.

* * *

Ty sprinted for the house when he saw smoke pouring from the front window.

"What's going on?" Shania called from the car.

Ty didn't answer as he fished in his pockets for his keys.

"Ty, what's wrong?"

Ty opened the door and ran inside, following the smoke to the kitchen. His dad sat calmly at the table as smoke from the microwave filled the room. "What happened?" Ty asked.

Ty's father said nothing, just pointed to the smoking microwave. Ty opened the door and more smoke poured out. Inside were the remains of something wrapped in foil.

"Dad, I told you not to—" Ty started, but

Shania's gasps cut him off.

"What's all of this?" Shania asked as she stood at the kitchen door, her eyes scanning the room covered in yellow Post-it notes.

"He can't remember things." Ty opened the front door to let more smoke out.

"What kind of things?" Shania asked in a tone Ty didn't like or need.

Ty stared outside, wishing he was anywhere else. "Anything."

00

"So are you going to ask me?" Shania asked Ty in an almost angry whisper.

Ty didn't like her tone—she'd used that ticked-off tone a lot lately—but was glad she finally spoke to him. Libraries were supposed to be quiet places, but Shania was taking it too far. When Ty showed up late for a study session, she'd frozen him out worse than a Detroit winter.

"Ask you what?" he countered. She still had her earbuds in; he could hear the bass boom.

Shania shook her head, smacked her gum, and buried her face back in her algebra book.

"Ask you what?" Ty repeated.

She didn't look up, blink an eye, or move a muscle.

Ty reached over, ripped the buds out of her ears, slammed the book shut, and pushed it off the table in the small study room. It landed on the floor with a thud. "What's your problem, Shania?"

She stood up and fixed Ty with an icy glare. "You."

"Me?"

Shania pushed past Ty, tears streaking her face, leaving her books and bags behind. Ty knew he should say something, maybe run after her, but he couldn't move. It felt like the walls of the small study room had closed in on him.

Ty picked up Shania's book, put it back on the table, and used it as pillow. But before his eyes shut, his phone rang. Not Shania, but his dad. Again.

Before he picked up, Ty steadied himself like he was on the foul line with the game on his shoulders. Every minute of every day felt that way since his dad had come home. Or rather, since the man who used to be his father took over his house.

"Hey, Dad." Ty's hello was clipped, the tone familiar. It was the one Shania had started using with him.

"When are you coming home?"

Ty laughed to himself at Shania's vacated bags and books. He fished in his wallet for his bus pass since Shania had driven them to the library. "Sooner than I thought."

"The alarm on my phone won't stop going off."

Like he'd learned in Teen ACHIEVE, Ty had programmed his dad's phone to remind him when it was time to take a med. Every med was laid out, labeled, but even that was too much.

He'd shown his dad over and over how to turn off the alarm.

"It makes my head hurt."

"I'll be home soon," Ty said with a sigh. Again, he'd disappoint one person to help another. *Balance*, he thought. But Ty knew this wasn't the kind of balance he needed in his life.

After hanging up with his father, Ty tried Shania, but she wouldn't pick up. He texted her, asking her to come back to the room, but she didn't reply. He tried to study, but the numbers and letters in the algebra book were squiggles on a page that made no sense.

Frustrated, angry, and more than a little scared, Ty gathered his things and started out of the room, but Shania was waiting for him outside, leaning against the wall.

"You were supposed to ask me to the Valentine's Day dance, Boo." Ty could tell by the scratching voice and red eyes she'd been crying. "Or maybe you don't want to go."

"I forgot. I'm sorry." Ty reached out for

Shania, but she turned her back.

"You can't treat me like this."

"Look, with my dad home, there's a lot to do. You saw my dad, the notes. You saw what my house looks like." He'd tried explaining it to Shania before. She'd just nod her head, saying she understood, but he knew she didn't. Couldn't.

"I have to go." He reached for Shania, but she dodged him.

Ty glanced at his phone and wished he had a contact for Malayeka. *She would understand,* Ty thought. *Like me, she's collateral damage of the war.*

02

"Henderson, get up!" Ty heard Coach Carlson yell from the bench, even over the cheering of the Southfield Chiefs' crowd as they applauded another Warren Wildcats turnover.

The buzzer sounded like a laser as Rondell Henderson ran onto the court, all smiles. "Nice game, Tyshawn," Rondell said as he passed Ty to replace him on the court. Ty offered a high five, but he couldn't tell from Rondell's tone if he was sincere or sarcastic. Given that Ty had more turnovers than points, the only person who thought Ty had a good game was probably the Chiefs' coach.

Ty took a towel from the bench, a bench he wasn't used to sitting on for longer than a few minutes, but with his game broken, he knew that more splinters in the butt were in his future.

"Let's work out there!" Coach Carlson yelled. The rest of the team shouted encouragement, but Ty couldn't bring himself to fake enthusiasm. Just months ago, he'd been a hero with his dad's image up on a big screen. Now, he sat at the end of the bench, his dad's needs looming like a dark cloud over his life.

* * *

"Tyshawn, I need you! Come here!" Ty hadn't even closed the front door all the way before his dad yelled for help. On the bus from Southfield, Ty sat alone, pushing away Arquavis, Rondell, and even Coach Carlson. He needed time to process what he'd lost: his minutes on the court, his grades, and hours upon hours of sleep. If he didn't get it together, he could add lost time with Shania to the list.

"I'm busy!" Ty shouted as he raced downstairs.

"No, I need you to—"

"I don't want to hear it!"

"Tyshawn, what's wrong?"

Ty answered his dad by slamming the basement door hard enough that a basketball trophy toppled from a shelf to the floor, breaking in half. "Leave me alone!" Ty yelled at his father. He wanted to shout it at everybody else who wanted more than he could give.

But Ty's father wouldn't back down. He pounded on the door over and over. "Tyshawn, I need you."

"I need—" Ty stopped. He didn't know how to finish the sentence. More hours in a day? Fewer responsibilities? To go back to how things were before?

The pounding on the door grew louder then

suddenly stopped. Ty opened the door and saw his father staring down, massaging his hands. "It hurts too much."

Ty looked down.

"I'm sorry this is all on you," his dad said.

"It's not your fault."

"I was on point," his dad mumbled. "It was my fault."

"Don't say that. It doesn't help anything."

"A man takes responsibility, Tyshawn." He continued to rub his hands.

Ty put his right hand on his dad's shoulder. "I'm not on point anymore. I lost my job to Rondell. I'm sorry I let you down. I can't concentrate anymore. I don't know what's wrong."

"It's not the end of the world."

"I worked all these years to start, and I lost it. It's not fair."

"Fair?" Ty's father said. "Come with me," and he wheeled into the living room. Ty obeyed.

Ty took the couch while his father pulled a DVD from a drawer below the TV, loaded it into the player, and turned the TV on.

"One of my therapists in the hospital in Germany gave this to me. To help me remember."

AFG:ISAFKUNAR:8/18/13 appeared in bold letters on the screen.

"What's that mean?" asked Ty. He leaned forward on the couch.

"This is footage from Afghanistan, 'Afg.' I was part of the International Security Assistance Force or ISAF in the Kunar province. The numbers show the date."

Then came grainy, black-and-white footage of soldiers, walking a street, guns drawn.

"We had intel that as many as forty insurgents had gathered, and we had to find them. We did a house-to-house search with drone backup, eyes in the sky."

At 2:12 into the footage, Ty's dad paused the scene, "See that big cloud in the corner? It was a booby-trapped door, and I opened it. That cloud is from the bomb that made me what I am now."

Ty was stunned. "Why didn't you show me this before?" he asked.

"Because it's too hard to watch, Ty. But you needed to know the truth tonight." Ty saw tears in his dad's eyes.

"You don't need to be left alone to struggle, Ty. Whatever happened tonight, you got tomorrow to make it better and the day after," his dad said. "I hope nothing in your life will ever be as bad as that cloud was to me. I'm giving you a gift, Son. It's called perspective."

13

"You haven't been creative in a while, have you?" asked Malayeka.

Ty stared at the box of crayons and bottles of glitter glue. "But this is like kindergarten, man." If it was kindergarten, Ty thought, at least there would be naptime.

Mr. Gomez overheard. "Not quite, Ty."

The circle of chairs for Teen ACHIEVE was now several tables, each with a box of craft items.

"It's art therapy," said Mr. Gomez, "It's a chance to reach inside ourselves for messages we can find no other way but through art."

"Reach inside for what?" Ty asked.

Malayeka reached across the table and placed her hand over Ty's hand. He wondered if she felt his pulse skip a beat when she touched him. She'd been gluing cotton balls to a page of yellow paper. "Usually, you don't know until you try." She pulled her hand away. "Trust me."

Mr. Gomez walked to another table where Queen and Tori had taken charge.

Ty leaned in. "Listen, I'm on the outs with Coach, my grades are dropping—"

"And you're having trouble taking care of your dad, you told us." Malayeka pushed the page of construction paper closer to him and finished his sentence. "Once you start this, you might like it."

Ty grabbed an orange crayon and started coloring on the page hard.

"Not like that," said Malayeka.

Ty dropped the crayon. "So I'm worried about leaving my dad alone to come here and color, okay?"

"I wish I could leave my mom alone," said Malayeka.

Ty paused. "What do you mean?"

"My mom never came back."

Ty swallowed. "You mean—"

"She died. So, yeah, I'd give everything to be able to take care of her."

He watched as tears welled up in her eyes. "I'm sorry," said Ty.

"It's alright. My family's strong. I'm strong. What Mr. Gomez has taught me really helped." She picked up the crayon and placed it in Ty's hand. "Show me you're strong."

Ty turned the page over. His father needing him was not as bad as not having his father alive. It was a scary thought.

He leaned in with the crayon. In his mind, he pictured the assignment—"draw what you want your future to look like"—and started to sketch.

After five minutes, he picked up another color and drew more. As he did, he forgot everything else—Coach, grades, girls, his father. He used another color, then another.

After twenty minutes, he was working the edges of the paper when Malayeka reached out to touch his hand again. "Hey, you got lost in this, didn't you?"

Ty stopped. "I guess I did."

Mr. Gomez came over. "Very nice, Ty. You want to share your drawing with the group?"

Ty stood up as Malayeka smiled. "This is how I see the future." He turned the page over to show a large fist surrounded by blue and orange bolts of lightning.

"And it means?" asked Mr. Gomez.

Ty looked at Malayeka. "It means strength, being strong."

Malayeka and Ty strolled the long lobby of the Vet Center as they talked. "Your drawing was really good."

"Fists are a theme for my dad and me. But fists used for good, not for bad," said Ty.

"What do you mean, 'for good?'" asked Malayeka.

"It's in every Bruce Lee movie. He has all this energy and potential, but he never uses his fists for bad reasons."

Malayeka stopped. "You're kidding me. The 'absorb what is useful' guy, that Bruce Lee?"

"How'd you know?"

"It's one of my favorite lines," said Malayeka.

"Mine, too."

The two smiled.

Malayeka reached in her purse for pen and paper. She leaned against a window and wrote, then handed the paper to Ty.

"I'd be disappointed if you didn't call me."

She held Ty's hand. "My ride's out front, so I gotta go."

Ty stared at the ten perfect digits. More thunder. More lightning. Let it rain.

14

"What's she like?" Ty's dad asked. His dad always said "she." Ty guessed he couldn't remember Malayeka's name.

"She's my age, she's really pretty. Dresses nice," said Ty as he cleared dishes from the living room. While someone might say the same about Shania, it was more than looks. Shania was a cheerleader; Malayeka was a leader.

"She's lucky, too, if she's dating you." It was

like his dad had forgotten all about Shania. Sometimes, Ty wished he could, too.

"It's not like that. She just gave me her phone number. And I don't even know where I stand with Shania." Ty continued cleaning. The art therapy project and talk with Malayeka afterwards had given him new energy. "What do we do with this now?" he asked, holding the back of the empty wheelchair.

"We're donating it back. It's going to someone who needs it, see?" With that, Ty's father rose from the couch and eased into place behind the walker. Once steady, Ty's father jumped in place three times.

"Careful, Dad." Ty held his hands out as though to catch his father's fall. "Your physical therapist said no sudden movement."

"Don't worry, Son. I got strength." Ty's father sat back down. "What are you gonna do about Shania?"

Ty shrugged and reached into his pocket for his phone. No calls. In fact, she hadn't called in three days. "Shania just wants so much from me right now." He looked at her picture on his phone. "I think she wants a break. I know I need one."

Ty's father laughed. "My son's a player."

"I'm not a player, Dad. I just need to focus. Hey, I've got a few things I want to show you in the kitchen."

Ty's father followed as Ty opened the freezer. "These are your meals for the week, all labeled and stored."

There was a look of surprise on his father's face. "When did you have time to do this?"

"I got up early and made spaghetti," Ty said, pointing. "And in these tubs here, red beans and rice."

"My favorite!"

Ty led his father to the microwave. "See this red tape here? That's at the three-minute mark. Never ever go over three minutes, okay?"

"Gotcha."

"And here," Ty draped a belt with a cell

phone holster around his father's waist. "So you don't lose your phone, I came up with this."

Ty's father looked down at the belt. "Not too shabby."

The front door opened. It was Ty's mom.

"Honey." Ty's father lit up as he walked quickly to her—but his pace was too quick and he stumbled into a chair.

Ty lunged forward to help. "Dad, you alright?"

Ty's mother didn't move.

Ty looked up at her. "He's been walking for about two weeks." He tried not to smile, to reward her when she hadn't done anything. He was happy to see her, but he'd done all the heavy lifting.

"So I missed my husband's first steps."

Ty didn't like her tone, couldn't tell if she was really proud or being sarcastic.

She gripped her keys, looked around the room, and sighed way too loud. "I thought one of you might call to keep me in the loop."

"I tried calling for like four days," said Ty.

"I was probably in meetings. We got the Chrysler contract, so I've been busy."

Ty's father rolled into the chair and began massaging a hurt leg. "I think I tried calling, too, honey." He laughed. "It's on a note somewhere."

"I forgot the notes," Ty's mother laughed, more out of disgust than humor. "What's the belt for?"

"Ty made this so I won't lose my phone. My phone rings whenever I need to take medication. He made meals for the week, too, all stacked in the freezer."

Her shoulders dropped. She looked at Ty. "The more you do for him, the less he does for himself."

Ty thought of Mr. Gomez and the support group. "But he's got a brain injury, which means—"

"Which means he has to exercise it more!" Ty's mother reached for the strap on her purse. "I was gonna ask you guys to dinner, but I see things are taken care of. I'm heading back to work."

With that, she turned and left.

After the door slammed, Ty and his father looked at one another.

Ty's father broke the silence. "Have you seen your mother lately?"

Ty feared the intense encounter had somehow triggered more short-term memory loss. "Dad, she was just here!"

"I know, I was just pulling your leg." He adjusted himself in the seat. "It'll take time. She's used to Sergeant Denver Douglas, and I'm the furthest thing from a sergeant now."

Ty thought for a moment—about his grades, about Shania, about Coach Carlson, Rondell, and the rest of the team. He thought about his father—the meals, the medications, the doctor visits. His mom could turn it on and off, just walk in and out when she pleased. Ty wouldn't walk out on his dad, but he knew he had to start making tough choices. Something had to give.

15

"Teflon, you sure about this?" Rondell asked. Ty and Rondell took turns shooting free throws before practice. In the few minutes he'd played in his last game, Ty missed three shots from the field, two from the line, and, he knew, his one chance of ever starting again.

"I don't have much of a choice," Ty answered.

On the way to practice, Ty told Rondell his plan to quit the team. He just needed one last practice with more time of his butt on the bench than his Jordans on the floor to make it real.

"It's not 'cause I took your minutes?" Rondell asked, sounding embarrassed.

Ty bounced the ball several times before he shot. The ball fell short. "No."

"Look, guys look up to you, even if you're not starting," Rondell said. "I know it's no fun to ride the bench. I did it for years." He picked up the ball, set himself and shot. All net.

"It's just time." Ty spared him the details.

"You should re-think it."

Ty took the ball in his hands and studied it, just like he'd studied the patterns of the basement ceiling the night before. Unable to sleep, overwhelmed by stress and worry, he lay awake, listening to his dad's wheelchair hum and roll across the floor.

"I don't get it. You're like a hero around here," Rondell whispered. "You got game, good grades, the hottest girl. Most guys here would kill just to have *one* of those."

Ty knew what he meant, but his version of what a hero looked like had changed. A hero was someone bound to a metal chair in January and walking baby steps by February.

"Shoot the ball, Ty. You're gonna miss anyway," Arquavis shouted as he joined Ty and Rondell at the foul line. Arquavis laughed so loud, it hurt Ty's ears as much as his pride.

Ty bounced the ball just once and took aim. The ball sailed through the air. No backboard, no rim, no net. Nothing but wood floor as the ball fell inches short. Ty could tell that Arquavis wasn't the only one mocking him, but Ty didn't want to see his teammates laughing faces. Head down, hiding his eyes and studying the wood grain, he mumbled, "I'm done."

* * *

"I won't allow it," Coach Carlson said. Ty sat next to him on the bench as the other players practiced. He'd told Coach he was quitting, but Coach wasn't having it.

"Look, I just don't want to play anymore."

"Don't give me that. You've played your entire life. It's in your blood."

Ty didn't argue. Ball was his blood, his skin, and his bones. It held him together.

"You don't want to be a quitter," Coach said. "That's the worst thing in the world."

"I just can't—"

Coach cut him off. "Do you know what the word *resilient* means?"

Ty thought he knew, but couldn't stand to be wrong. "No," he answered.

"Resilient means you're strong in hard times, that you bounce back from adversity."

Ty kept his head down. Sounds of his teammates shooting, dribbling, and laughing filled the gym. They were the sounds he wanted in his life, not the beeping of machines. "I guess."

"Ty . . . I can only imagine how much pressure you're under, with school and your dad at home and all. This is the hardest test you'll face in high school," said Coach. He leaned in close and put an arm on Ty's shoulder. "Show me—show yourself—you're resilient."

Coach handed him a ball. "Look, you can control the ball even if you can't get your hands around it. Life's the same. You have it in you. Don't let me down."

Ty bounced the ball against the hardwood. He loved that sound. He'd heard it most of his life and couldn't imagine life without it. He felt like he'd let his mom down, or else she'd be at home. He'd let his dad down every day in some way. "Coach, I don't know what to do."

16

FEBRUARY 7 / THURSDAY, LATE AFTERNOON
TYSHAWN'S HOUSE

"You made the right call," Rondell said. Even though he lived a few blocks away from Ty, he'd walked with him all the way home. "Trust me, wearing that uniform is an honor in itself."

Ty let Rondell do most of the talking, just like he'd let Rondell and Coach Carlson talk him out of quitting the team. It wasn't that he felt strong, like Coach said, but that he felt too weak to stand up for himself. *I gotta find me again*, Ty thought.

"What's going on at your house?" Rondell asked as they rounded the corner. Ty's father stood at the top of the ramp, a skateboard under each arm. In the driveway shoveling snow was Demonte, while Benj hacked away at ice in the gutters.

"I told 'em if they want to play, they gotta pay," Ty's dad shouted over the racket.

"You can tell he was in the Army," Ty said to Rondell, laughing. "He likes giving orders."

"I better bounce before he's got me building a snowman," Rondell said as he walked off.

"Demonte, what's up?" He didn't know Demonte or Benj that well. They took the bus together, jaw-jacked about nothing, and skated on his ramp, but that was about it. Ty just didn't hang out with skaters much.

"What's it look like?" Demonte answered. "I'm doing your job!"

"I can't believe my dad made you two—"

"Nah, we kinda volunteered," Demonte said. "We're used to it." Ty knew that, like Benj, Rondell, and half the guys he knew, Demonte had no father at home. They'd become man of the house before they learned to shave.

"'Sides, looks like you could use the help," said Benj as he climbed off the ladder and walked to Ty and Demonte.

"Thanks, guys," Ty said.

"Benj wants to help you with something else, I bet," Demonte laughed.

"With what?" Ty answered as his "to-do" list ran like movie credits in his mind.

"Take out Shania," Demonte cracked.

Ty pretended to laugh. He pulled his phone from his pocket to look at all the calls from Shania. None, which was way worse than twenty of them.

"So, what's your dad's story?" Benj asked.

Ty held his phone in his hand, his finger hovering over Shania's number. Ty looked at his phone, at the porch, and at the snow-free drive-way. "He was on patrol . . ." Ty began.

* * *

"You're breaking up with me over the phone?" Ty asked Shania. After Benj and Demonte heard his dad's story and paid their propers, Ty finally called Shania. Like she'd done the past week, she refused to answer until Ty left her a plead-ing voicemail. "Shania, seriously?"

"I got plenty of guys who wanna get with me," Shania said. "You're like a ghost."

Ty had liked being called "Boo" more than a ghost. But he wasn't sure what to say. "I'm sorry."

"Don't cut it no more."

Ty lay back on his bed in the basement. Upstairs, he could hear his dad pushing the walker, moving from room to room.

"I just got so much going on," Ty said, rat-tling off his responsibilities.

She cut him off. "I thought you were quit-ting the team." It had been her idea.

"I tried, but I couldn't. Ball is my life."

"I thought I was your life. That's what you're supposed to say. You gotta be telling me, 'Shania, you're the most important thing in my life.'"

Ty was silent.

"So, that's what I thought," Shania said.

"I need your help, Ty!" Ty's dad yelled from the top of the stairs. He sounded frantic.

"You got nothing to say?" Shania snapped. "Seems to me—"

Ty ended the call and started up the stairs, feeling his burden a little lighter.

07

Ty stepped from his car in the school parking lot. Taking the bus saved on gas, but now that he was his dad's main caregiver, he'd asked his mom for more gas money. She gave him a gas card instead, as though she didn't trust him.

Ty's phone hummed in his pocket during Mr. Murry's class. In the middle of a class reading assignment, everyone around him could hear it buzzing.

A minute later, his phone hummed again.

"Man, you gonna get that phone, Ty?" asked Demonte. "It's hard to concentrate."

Mr. Murry spoke from the desk. "What's going on?"

Ty reached into his pocket. "It's my phone, Mr. M. Somebody's trying—"

"Ty, you know my rule about phones in class," he said as he walked toward Ty.

Ty punched the buttons. It was a voicemail message from a nurse at St. John's Hospital. "Please reach us. It's about your father."

Ty jumped from his seat. "Mr. M., it's the hospital. Something's wrong with my dad."

With that, he stuffed his books under his arms and headed for the door.

"Check in with the office before you leave," said Mr. Murry, but Ty was already out the door and heading down the hall, running faster than he'd ever run in his life.

* * *

The woman behind the hospital information desk couldn't move fast enough. "What was the name again?" she asked.

"Denver. Denver Douglas," Ty said quickly. He needed information, and he needed it fast.

"I don't have a listing for a Denver. That's the last name, right?"

"No—Douglas is the last name."

The woman adjusted her glasses as she looked at the screen. "Oh, I found him," she wrote on a piece of paper. She looked up. "Are you over the age of eighteen?"

"No, but I do everything for him—where is he? Can I see him?"

The woman handed the note to Ty. "If you'll have a seat in the lobby, I'll have someone from social services come down and talk to you."

"How long is that gonna take?" Ty asked, trying not to shout.

"Someone from social services will be right down. Just have a seat."

Ty was stumped. He was finally in the same

building as his father, but he couldn't see him and still didn't know what was going on.

He looked around the room. There were whole families, sitting, just like him, but no one alone. What was wrong with his father? What had happened?

He reached for his phone and pushed a button.

"This is Nicolette Douglas. Please leave a message, and I'll return your call."

It was no surprise his mother didn't pick up. She answered maybe one in ten of Ty's calls. Ty wondered if she was avoiding the message or him, the messenger. He left a message anyway. "Mom, it's me, Ty. I'm at the hospital with Dad. Please call."

He set the phone on his knee. A moment later, he reached for his wallet and pulled out another piece of paper. He paused and then dialed.

"Hello?"

The sound of her voice poured warmly over him. "Hey, Malayeka, you doing anything?"

"Tyshawn!" He could hear the smile in her

voice. "I'm just out of school. What's up?"

"I'm at the emergency room at St. John's in Warren. It's my dad."

Without missing a beat, Malayeka said fiercely, "I'm on my way."

A few minutes later, a middle-aged white woman with short black hair approached Ty. "Are you Tyshawn?" she said, her hand outstretched.

"That's me."

"I'm Mrs. McKay from social services. Let's go to a consult room so we can talk."

Ty followed her down a hallway into a small room. She shut the door behind her.

"Tyshawn, your dad had a seizure this morning."

Ty blinked. "Seizure?"

"Thankfully, it happened during physical therapy, so he was brought here for testing."

Ty still didn't have enough information. "Will he be ok?"

"It depends. There are medications to help,

and there will be follow-up testing. But you need to know," she said, reaching across the table to touch Ty's shaking hand, "your dad told me what a strong young man you are and how well he's being taken care of. He's bragged about you all afternoon."

Ty looked down and smiled.

She pulled her hand away. "We have the best neurologists here. When he's through with testing, we'll go up and see him together."

"They'll let me in, even though I'm not eighteen?"

"They'll let you in because I'm gonna *tell* them to let you in, how's that?"

The two headed back to the emergency room waiting area when Ty saw Malayeka. She wore her blue-and-white Cass Tech school uniform.

"I'll be back soon," Mrs. McKay said as she walked away.

Ty stopped. Seeing Malayeka was by far the best thing that had happened to him in a long while. He felt a wave of relief come over him.

Malayeka smiled and began to walk toward him. When the two met up, they hugged one another hard, as if they'd been doing it for years.

"Thanks for coming," whispered Ty.

"Sure. This kind of thing—you don't have to go it alone."

"There's so much—" Ty said, even though he knew Malayeka understood.

"It's going to work out," she said softly, yet firmly.

"I don't know where to begin," Ty said. Malayeka pointed to a row of chairs, and Ty followed her.

"Why is your dad here?" she asked. Hospital beeps, families crying, phones ringing, and muffled announcements filled the silence as Ty gathered his thoughts.

"They say he had a seizure, and—"

"No," Malayeka interrupted, "tell me the whole story."

Ty took a deep breath like he was at the foul line in a tie game with one second on the clock. Malayeka leaned in, placing her small hand just an inch from Ty's. "He was on patrol . . ."

18

"Great pass, Rondell!" Ty shouted out at the court. Rondell's perfect pitch to Arquavis set a lay-up, which put the Wildcats ahead by 20 going into the final quarter.

Ty tossed Rondell a towel. As he watched Rondell wipe away the sweat, Ty remembered the final game of the holiday tourney when he'd soaked up the crowd's cheers like a sponge. It was only two months ago, but it felt like a different lifetime.

"Douglas, up!" Coach Carlson yelled. "You're in for Henderson. Make it count."

Ty nodded and took a deep breath. As he ran onto the court, he glanced into the stands. Malayeka sat with Queen and Tori, the girls from Teen ACHIEVE.

"You remember how to pass the ball, Douglas?" Arquavis cracked. "Seems to me you play more like iron than Teflon." Ty said nothing, letting the cheers of the crowd wash over him. Shania was leading them—she could cheer for Arquavis now. Ty was fine with Rondell taking his minutes on the court, but Arquavis pouncing on Shania was too much.

Ty took the ball from the ref and stood out of bounds. The whistle blew, and Wildcats scattered across the court, dogged by Brighton Bears. Ty head-faked left, inbounded right.

Arquavis gathered up Ty's perfect pass and started up court. Ty raced behind and set up near half court. The ball came back to Ty; he was back on point.

With the Bear guard growling in his face, Ty passed to Jamal, the Wildcat center, at the top of the key. Jamal pivoted, faked a shot, passed the ball back, and then set a screen. Ty took the ball, but only for a second as Arquavis cut for the basket. Ty tossed the pass high and hard between the defenders into Arquavis's hands, who laid it off the backboard into the net.

* * *

"Great hands, LeBron!" Benj joked when Ty dropped the Big Mac Benj had thrown to him.

"I like your hands just fine," Malayeka whispered in Ty's ear. She sat next to him in a crowded McDonald's booth. Queen, Tori, Demonte and Benj jammed in next to them.

"Maybe I'll teach you how to pass," Ty countered.

"And maybe I'll teach you how to skate that ramp like a champ," Benj said.

"And maybe—" Demonte jumped in the

conversation. Back and forth they went, taking shots at Ty. How friends talk.

Ty sat back in his seat as Malayeka held onto his arm. "It seems like everybody's getting along just fine. I told you it would work out," she whispered.

"You always say that," Ty whispered back. He had never met anyone as confident or optimistic as Malayeka. Or maybe it was something else, that word Coach had used. *Resilient.*

"How's your dad?" Malayeka asked. She always asked; Shania never had.

Even with bright lights and laughter all around him, Ty felt darkness. He hesitated. "You ever study mythology, Greek gods?" Ty asked.

Malayeka shrugged.

"There's this guy called Sisyphus who pissed off Zeus," Ty explained. He loved the Greek heroes for the same reason he loved Bruce Lee: in the end, they always won. "So as punishment, Zeus made him push a big rock up a hill, but right when it gets to the top, it rolls back down."

Malayeka held Ty's arm tighter.

"That's my life, my dad's life now."

"Is there anything I can do?" Malayeka pressed her head against Ty's shoulder.

Tyshawn looked over at her. "Just be on the hill with me."

19

"Mom, it's not like that. He can walk now." Ty felt Malayeka squeeze his hand for support.

"*He fell into a chair.*" Ty's mom sounded overwhelmed, even over the phone.

"He's getting better. They say his seizure was probably due to the medications he's taking, that he might have missed one or something. It's a small setback. And someone comes by to clean and do stuff for him. He's better. You should come home."

"I'm buried in this Chrysler contract. I can't risk it."

"Not even one evening?"

There was a pause. "I'll think about it. Listen, where are you now?"

"I'm at the Vet Center. There's a support group I've been going to."

"So *you're* going to therapy?"

"It's not therapy, it's more like—"

"See, this is what bothers me. You're not the one having the problem, and you're going to a support group?"

"But it's—"

"Your dad used to be strong. If he just didn't have everyone taking care of him, he'd get better faster."

"And he is, Mom."

Another pause. "Sorry, I've got someone from Chrysler in the lobby."

Ty listened to the silence on his phone. "Mom? Mom?"

Malayeka put her arm around his shoulder. "Remember what Mr. Gomez said: work on the things you can control." She looked in his eyes. "I'll help you push the rock."

The two walked into Teen ACHIEVE and took seats next to Mr. Gomez. Going on six meetings now, Ty felt he was among the older, wiser members of the group like Malayeka, who'd been coming to the group for months.

Mr. Gomez opened the group and then asked each teen to discuss events from the past week. First to speak was a newcomer, Danielle, who talked about how much she and her younger sister missed their father.

Ty raised his hand, and Mr. Gomez called on him.

"I didn't know about this until I came to the group," said Ty, "but if you bring in a photo of your dad, the auxiliary here has a printer where they'll print your father's photo on a pillow-case. Might be something you can look into for your sister."

Malayeka squeezed Ty's hand.

"Great recommendation, Ty," said Mr. Gomez.

A new guy named Jermaine told how hard it was to concentrate at school, that watching the news every night—the bombs, the wounded, the gunfire—had him worrying all the time.

Ty raised his hand. Again Mr. Gomez called on him.

"You should be here next time we have art therapy. Mr. Gomez, when is that?" He saw Jermaine's raised eyebrow as Mr. Gomez responded, and he jumped back in. "I know, art therapy sounds kind of . . . I don't know. It's good, though. And have you tried writing stuff down, like the things you're thinking and worrying about during the day? It seems like busy work, but it really helps."

Mr. Gomez's nodded at Ty and smiled. "Thank you for that contribution. As Ty mentioned, when we have feelings we don't express, they come out some way—sometimes in anger, sometimes in depression."

This time, Jermaine nodded knowingly.

"You have to find a way to express yourself," said Mr. Gomez, "and journaling or art therapy, those are both good ways."

* * *

Ty and Malayeka found themselves strolling the long hallway of the Veterans Center again after the group meeting.

"Right here," said Malayeka. "This is where I gave you my number, right?"

Ty looked around. "I believe it was."

With that, Malayeka punched him softly in the arm. "So why'd it take so long to call?"

Ty put his arms around her waist. "I had stuff to take care of. You know how busy I've been."

Malayeka smiled. "I know. But things are getting better, aren't they?"

"If I could just convince my mom of that."

"What did she say when you called?"

"She's still on this kick about 'Dad won't get better unless you leave him alone.'"

"Isn't he already getting better?"

"Lots better. But how will she know if she doesn't even stop by and visit?"

The two continued, walking in silence. Ty thought about the group and what a great feeling it was to have helpful things to say. Then he thought about his mom and how, try as he could, he couldn't get her to come home. A thought then crossed his mind. If he brought in her picture, he could have it copied on a pillowcase for his dad. Ty laughed aloud.

"What's so funny?" asked Malayeka.

"I may have to take my own advice."

20

MARCH 14 / SATURDAY AFTERNOON
TYSHAWN'S HOUSE

"I thought he was better," Ty's mom whispered, glancing inside as Ty greeted her at the door. Ty had invited her to dinner to meet Malayeka, but his mom was more concerned with her husband when she saw that he was in a wheelchair.

"He overdid it the other day," said Ty. She didn't need to know the details. "He's learning he can't to do too much at one time. Just like he coached me, balance in all things."

"Not everybody grows up with Bruce Lee as a father," she laughed.

Ty couldn't remember the last time he'd seen her smile or laugh, but it was too long ago.

"Mom, this is Malayeka," Ty said, glancing her way with pride. "She goes to Cass Tech. You know, the team I personally crushed in the holiday tournament?"

Malayeka stepped from behind Ty's father. "Nice to meet you."

"I hope for everyone's sake you did the cooking," said Ty's mom. "I wouldn't trust either of them."

"Hey, I've gotten to be pretty good at cooking," said Ty.

"And at ordering pizza," joked Ty's dad.

"Why don't we all have a seat?" Ty's mom said, pointing toward the living room.

"Already got one." Ty's father tilted his chair up like a kid doing a wheelie on a bike.

Ty's mom took a seat in her usual chair. Ty took a seat on the couch, gently pulling

Malayeka to his side. His dad did most of the talking, while Ty did most of the eating. Ty noticed his mom wasn't saying much, not even questioning Malayeka like a cop with a suspect, which is how she treated every other girl Ty had brought home. Ty sensed an odd vibe in the room. It was like one of those puzzle pictures where everything looked normal, but when you looked closer, stuff was wrong.

After an awkward silence, Ty's mom finally spoke. "I have good news and bad news. That Chrysler contract? They gave it to another vendor, so I told the company I was taking a few days off to be with my family."

"Honey, I'm sorry," said Ty's dad.

"I didn't lose my job or anything like that. In fact, I think it's a good thing. Contracts can come and go, right? But not family." She paused, and her face softened as she looked at Ty's father. "I found out the hard way."

Malayeka smiled. "That sounds like something my father would say."

Ty grabbed Malayeka's hand. "Malayeka was in the stands at the city tournament."

"You saw the big play?"

"I did. Too bad it took your son three months to call me." She nudged Ty.

Ty started to protest, but Malayeka cut him off. "But you know what else I saw that day?"

"What was that?" asked Ty's mom.

Malayeka's gaze turned toward Ty's father. "I saw a hero."

* * *

After dinner, Ty and Malayeka put the dishes away, stealing kisses when they could. Ty stayed quiet, apart from the clanking of plates, listening in. When Malayeka started to ask Ty something, he stopped her and pointed toward the living room, where his parents sat and talked.

"I wanted the Denver I knew," his mom said, "The Denver I fell in love with in school."

"I've always been here, honey," Ty's father insisted. "We had a little setback, that's all."

"I know that in my head, but in my heart . . . We dealt with setbacks before, but this, this—" Ty's mom paused, then leaned forward. "Denver, are you *really* doing better?"

Looking into the room, Ty thought his dad seemed hurt by the question, but then a smile returned to his face. "I'll show you. Ty?" he called.

Ty stepped back into the room and motioned for Malayeka to join him. "Yeah?"

After taking a deep breath, Ty's father pushed himself up from his wheelchair, grunting with the effort. Once he stood, he reached out for his wife's hand. "Everybody, time for hoops."

Slowly, Ty's dad made it out the front door, his wife by his side. *That's how it should be*, Ty thought. Instead of walking down the ramp, Ty's dad sluggishly made his way down the steps. From inside the garage, he grabbed a basketball. "Dad, what are you doing?" Ty asked as he handed it over.

"I got this," Ty's father said with a confidence that Ty hadn't heard in a while. Ty's father bounced the ball off the pavement, slowly at first, then faster, harder until he got to a yellow line painted on the driveway. "Three pointer?" Ty's dad took a half-step, planted his foot and shot. The ball clanked the rusted hoop and then fell in.

Malayeka and Ty laughed. Ty saw his mom wasn't laughing; she looked stunned.

Ty's father grabbed the ball as it bounced back. He turned quickly to his wife. "Layup?" He took three slow steps and jumped, bouncing the ball against the backboard and into the net.

Retrieving the ball again, he turned to his wife, a little winded. "You asked if I really am doing better, yes. You just haven't been around to see."

Ty nodded and put an arm around his mom. He and Malayeka were still laughing at his father's showing off, but his mom started to cry. Ty was glad it was not because she'd lost something, but rather because something she'd lost had been found.

20

"Drive, Demonte, drive to the basket!" Ty's dad shouted. Demonte gathered in Rondell's pass and then made his way to the basket, forgetting to dribble. "Travel!"

"You travel so much, you should get frequent flyer miles," Ty cracked.

Demonte tossed the ball to Ty. It fell inches short. Ty and Benj were up by two against Rondell and Demonte with Ty's dad yelling orders like a drill instructor.

"I ain't never gonna get the hang of this," Demonte said, almost in a pout.

"You'd be surprised what you can learn," said Ty's dad. "Never give up on yourself."

For a minute, the only sound among the five was Ty bouncing the ball. Behind him, the soundtrack of games on nearby courts—blocked shots, trash talk, slam dunks—seemed louder than normal. Finally, Ty broke the silence as he passed the ball to his dad. "Dad, you prove that every day."

His father caught the ball, bounced it twice, and passed it back. "You, too, Ty. You, too."

"I gotta get to the dentist after hanging out with you two," Demonte cracked. "You're all givin' me more cavities than a bag of candy."

Ty felt the blood rushing to his face. He put the ball in front of him.

"Demonte, you best not be trash talkin' if you can't bring game," Rondell said.

"We play ball with you, you skate with us,

that's the deal?" Benj pointed at the skateboards resting in the grass. "Ty, let's see how good you and Rondell are on wheels."

"I can teach you something about that," said Ty's dad as he popped a wheelie with his chair. Ty knew why his dad was back in his wheelchair. He had pushed himself too hard with the exercises his physical therapist recommended, but that was the Denver Douglas way. With time and patience, his dad would be back with the walker, then walking again.

Ty looked at his friends. They all looked like they wanted to laugh at the wheelchair trick but didn't know if they should, so Ty went on point.

"Good one, Dad."

Ty's dad laughed the loudest. But the laughter gave way to noise from a nearby court. Ty recognized one voice among the chaos: Arquavis. Since Arquavis hooked up with Shania, he and Ty hadn't spoken, other than on the court and only when necessary. Now that the season was over, with the Wildcats eliminated in the first round of playoffs, Ty didn't need to maintain his silence or the peace.

"Where you going, Ty?" Benj yelled as Ty started toward the other court. His walk turned into a run, ending in a full out sprint.

"Arquavis!" Ty shouted as he closed in. Arquavis and three other players, older guys he vaguely remembered from school, stopped their game. Jamal was on the bench, looking at his phone.

"Hey, guys, you remember Tyshawn Douglas," Arquavis said, smiling. "He used to be starting point guard. He used to have the hottest girlfriend, but used to don't count for much."

"That's what you'd like to think." Ty stared at Arquavis, who stared back. Neither blinked.

"He wants everybody to feel sorry for him 'cause his dad got all messed up in the war."

"I don't want anything from you Arquavis," Ty countered. "Except an apology."

Arquavis faced Ty as he talked, but his audience was the other players on the court. "If you're talking about Shania—"

"I know you talked her into breaking up with me."

"How she tells it, you weren't that into her," Arquavis said. His buds laughed. Ty wanted to counter, to tell the truth, but not around strangers. "You're just a loser, Tyshawn."

"Let's go, you and me, one on one!" Ty shouted in Arquavis's face. But before Arquavis could answer, Ty heard a noise behind him followed by Rondell's voice.

"You don't need to go it alone, Teflon," Rondell said. "You got a team."

"I see one player, one loser, and two skaters. You're four players short of a team," laughed Arquavis.

"Five players is a team, and I'm on point." Ty heard his dad say as he turned around. The wheelchair moved roughly across the pitted pavement. "Now, gimme that ball."

Arquavis tossed the ball hard and high, but Ty's dad caught it with ease. He bounced the ball rhythmically. It sounded like the marching of boots, the beating of a heart.

"Serious?" Arquavis said. His friends all laughed, except Jamal.

"Serious," Ty's dad answered as he shot the ball to the net. The ball banged the backboard and fell through the hoop. "Basketball's one thing I didn't forget."

ABOUT THE AUTHORS

Patrick Jones is the author of more than twenty novels for teens. He has also written two nonfiction books about combat sports, *The Main Event*, on professional wrestling, and *Ultimate Fighting*, on mixed martial arts. He has spoken to students at more than one hundred alternative schools, including residents of juvenile correctional facilities. Find him on the web at www.connectingya.com and on Twitter @PatrickJonesYA.

A magazine editor for ten years, Brent Chartier has written three books for young adults. His interest in concussions stems from his work with the Center for Neurological Studies, Dearborn, MI. He lives in a Detroit suburb with his son, Casey, and their two cats.

**CHECK OUT ALL OF THE TITLES IN THE
SUPPORT AND DEFEND SERIES**

LOCKED OUT

Prisoners pay for their crimes by being locked up.
But what about their kids, who are locked out?

RETURNING TO NORMAL
PATRICK JONES

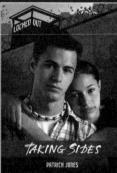
TAKING SIDES
PATRICK JONES

GUARDING SECRETS
PATRICK JONES

RAISING HEAVEN
PATRICK JONES

DOING RIGHT
PATRICK JONES

ALSO FROM AUTHOR PATRICK JONES